World of Reading 1

THIS IS KATE BISHOP: HAWKEYE

Adapted by **Megan Logan**

Illustrated by **Steve Kurth, Geanes Holland, and Olga Lepaeva**

Based on the Marvel comic book series **Hawkeye: Kate Bishop**

MARVEL
Los Angeles
New York

MARVEL

Printed in the United States of America
First Edition, September 2021
10 9 8 7 6 5 4 3 2 1
Library of Congress Control Number: 2021936356
FAC-029261-21211
ISBN: 978-1-368-07493-3

This is Kate Bishop.
She is Hawkeye.

Kate lives in Brooklyn. She loves her part of New York City.

Kate is friends with Clint Barton.
He is also Hawkeye.

Clint trains with Kate.
They work together.

Kate and Clint train to be ready for anything.

Kate and Clint keep each other on their toes.

Kate is skilled
with a bow and arrow.

Kate trains to fight.

She works hard.
She is strong.

Kate is a good teammate.

She doesn't need super-powers to be a good hero.

She wants to learn everything she can.

She learns that being a hero . . .

. . . is not always easy.

But every heroic act
is worth the effort.

A hero's work is never done.

Danger can strike at any time.

Kate is ready.
She can handle anything.

Even Tony Stark.

Kate depends on her friends.

And they depend on her.

They can do anything . . .

. . . together.

Kate is learning every day.

She is getting better every day.

Kate Bishop is Hawkeye!